Look Out! Look Out!
Tractor About

by Joan Dalgleish

illustrated by Pete Joison and Gordon Clarke

The Characters

Sid Baker
An old farmer

Jenny
Sid's trusty horse

Ken Baker
Sid's son

Keith Brown
The farmer next door

The Setting

CONTENTS

CHAPTER

Sid Needs a Tractor

Sid Baker and his horse, Jenny, had worked as a team for years.

They were friends.

Jenny pulled a plough that dug the earth. She walked along slowly while Sid spread the seed.

Sid's son, Ken, milked the cows.
He mended the fences.
He took the crops to market
in an old truck.

"Why don't you get a tractor, Dad?" Ken asked.
"Keith Brown has one."

"No," said his father.
"Good old Jenny will do me."

One day a man from the city
came to the farm. He laughed
at Jenny pulling the plough.

He showed Sid a photo
of a brand new tractor.

"Horses are too slow," he said.
"A tractor will do the work
in half the time."

"Go on Dad," said Ken.
"Our fences are down. Our cattle
are straying. You could use
the extra time to help me.
Why don't you buy a tractor?"

"I'll think about it,"
said his father.

"I'd have more time," he told Jenny.
"We could go for rides together.
Better than walking up and down the
same field all day, eh?"

Jenny blew in his ear.

CHAPTER  2

Sid Buys a Tractor

The tractor came on the back of a large truck.

"It's easier to drive than a horse.
No feed to mix, no coat to brush.
Just fill her up with diesel
and away she goes,"
said the driver.

Jenny watched as Sid drove off
on the new tractor.

It was noisy. Sid had to wear
ear plugs. The dogs barked at it.
Birds flew out of the trees.

Jenny neighed loudly
and trotted away in disgust.

The tractor ploughed the field
in half the usual time.

"Wonderful! Wonderful!" Sid cried.
"The best money I ever spent."

By midday he had ploughed
a second field. The sun was high
in the sky.

"Lunch time," he said,
and jumped off the tractor.
He forgot about the brake.
He forgot to turn the engine off.

"Whoa," he said, and walked away.

CHAPTER  3

Trail of Disaster

Chug. Chug. Chug. The tractor
moved off by itself. It went across
the field and into the next one.

21

It ran over a crop of young
corn plants. It squashed them flat.

Chug. Chug. Chug.
The tractor kept on going.
It went through a fence
and onto the road.

Some sheep were eating grass
on the side of the road. The noise
of the tractor made the sheep run.

It chased them down the road
and into the farm next door.

The tractor kept on going.

Keith Brown was taking some pumpkins to market. The pumpkins were piled high on the truck.

He drove around a bend.

"Aahh!" he yelled. "Look out!
Look out! Tractor about!"

Keith Brown swung the steering wheel.
The truck tipped over.

Hundreds of pumpkins bounced and rolled over the road.

He stopped the truck.
He was very angry.

"Look what you've done!" he cried.

He picked up a pumpkin.
He threw it at the tractor.
He shook his fist in the air.
"Come back here!"

Chug. Chug. Chug.
The tractor kept on going.
It bumped over a cattle grid
and into the farmyard.

The hens were scratching in the dust.
"Brark! Brark! Skwark! Skwark!"

They flew up in the air.
They flew sideways. They flew
all ways. The hens flapped and
cackled as the tractor scared
them all over the place.

The tractor kept going.

CHAPTER 4

The Tractor Comes Back

Sid's wife, Liz, was hanging out the washing.

"Aaah! Eeeek!"

The tractor ran right into the line of washing.

"Stop! Stop!" she cried.

The tractor kept on going,
taking the washing line with it.

Clothes flew from either side.
Shirts and jeans flapped in the wind.

"It's heading for the dam!"
cried Liz. She began to run.
"Look out! Look out! Tractor about!"

Sid had finished his lunch.
He walked outside and stretched
his arms into the air.

When Sid opened his eyes,
he saw his new tractor racing down
a bank towards the dam.

"Oh no!" he yelled.
"Who let my tractor loose?"

He began to run.

"Whoa! Whoa!" he cried. "Whooaa!!"

Chug. Chug. Chug. The tractor kept on going.

Ken was bending over,
fixing the water pump.

The tractor came closer,
and closer, and closer.

Ken was fastening the what-cha-
ma-call-it.

Bump!

Splash! Ken went head first into the dam.

Sid jumped up on the tractor.
At the very edge of the dam,
Sid made it stop.

Ken came up out of the water.
He laughed. "I almost got ploughed.
I'm glad you didn't dig **me** up."

Sid looked back over the path
of the runaway tractor.
He saw the broken washing line,
the cackling hens
and the smashed pumpkins.
He could see scattered sheep
and flat corn stalks.

"What a stupid tractor!" he said.

Ken and Liz looked at each other but did not say a word.

Then Sid remembered.
He was the one who had forgotten
to turn off the engine.
"Oh," he said. His face went red.

That night, Sid shut the tractor
in the shed. He took some carrots
to his horse.

"Sorry I'm late, Jenny," he said, patting her mane.
"I had to clean up the mess."

Jenny snorted into his hand as she ate the carrots.

"Well, old girl," said Sid. "A tractor can do the work in half the time, but by golly, it's double the trouble."

GLOSSARY

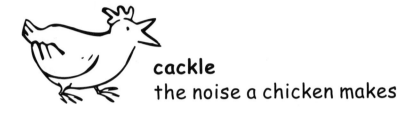

cackle
the noise a chicken makes

diesel
fuel for lorries
and tractors

disgust
strong dislike

grid
metal strips to
stop cattle

plough
a machine to dig up
the ground

runaway
moving without a driver

scatter
to go in all directions

Joan Dalgleish

Joan has had ten books published for children, including *Albert's Birthday* and *Dog on a Diet.* She loves visiting schools to talk about books and reading. She is a writer, actor and passionate walker.

Pete Joison and Gordon Clarke

These two run a graphic design studio. It's called Uddi Uddi and they create graphics that entertain. They each have one wife and one baby girl. Pete's favourite colour is cheesecake yellow and Gordon's favourite number is Pi. Life is good.